Princess Olivia

First published 2017 by Brown Watson
The Old Mill, 76 Fleckney Road
Kibworth Beauchamp
Leicestershire LE8 0HG

ISBN: 978-0-7097-2466-7
© 2017 Brown Watson, England
Printed in Malaysia

Brown Watson
ENGLAND

Princess Olivia was in her bedroom, surrounded by clothes. 'What are you doing?' asked the Queen. 'I am choosing a dress for my party,' replied Princess Olivia.

They looked at every dress in the pile, but none of them was quite right. 'Why don't you look in the garden for something pretty?' suggested the Queen. 'We can show your ideas to the royal dressmaker.'

Princess Olivia was excited.
She thought that was an excellent idea.
She ran into the royal gardens and looked
around. A little squirrel hopped past and
asked what she was doing.

'I need something pretty to decorate my new dress,' said the Princess. The squirrel hopped away, and returned with a shiny acorn. The Princess thought for a moment.

'No...it's too green,' said Princess Olivia.
'But thank you anyway.' The squirrel ran
across the grass to tell all of its friends.

Princess Olivia skipped to the flowerbed. A little rabbit scampered across the lawn, and dropped a daisy at her feet. 'Gosh, how kind!' said Princess Olivia, and thought for a moment.

'No...it's too simple,' said Princess Olivia.
'But thank you anyway.' The rabbit ran
across the grass and back to its burrow.

Princess Olivia wandered to the pond. A frog hopped up on a lily pad and offered her a flower. 'That's lovely!' said Princess Olivia, and thought for a moment.

13

'No...it's too big,' said Princess Olivia. 'But thank you anyway.' The frog croaked, and dived back into the water.

Princess Olivia gazed across the lawn.
A little hedgehog trundled over the grass,
with a pink flower perched on its prickles.
'How nice of you!' said Princess Olivia,
and thought for a moment.

'No...it's too bright,' said Princess Olivia.
'But thank you anyway.' The hedgehog
scampered across the lawn and back
to its pile of leaves.

Princess Olivia ambled to the meadow
at the edge of the garden. A friendly
pony trotted up to her with a sunflower
between its teeth. 'How lovely!' said
Princess Olivia, and thought for
a moment.

'No...it's too yellow,' said Princess Olivia.
'But thank you anyway.' The pony
nuzzled her hand and then galloped away.

Princess Olivia heard a soft hoot, and looked up into the trees. An owl blinked down at her, and plucked a berry from the tree. 'How kind!' said Princess Olivia, and thought for a moment.

'No...it's too shiny,' said Princess Olivia.
'But thank you anyway.' The owl flapped
its wings and flew silently off into
the forest.

Princess Olivia listened carefully.
She could hear a rustling in the
undergrowth. A tiny mouse jumped up
onto a log, and offered her a pinecone.
'How nice of you!' said Princess Olivia,
and thought for a moment.

'No...it's too brown,' said Princess Olivia. 'But thank you anyway.' The mouse jumped off the log and scampered down a hole.

Princess Olivia peered into the darkness of the forest. A deer tiptoed out from behind a tree, and offered her a holly branch. 'How kind!' said Princess Olivia, and thought for a moment.

'No...it's too spiky,' said Princess Olivia. 'But thank you anyway.' The deer turned tail and bobbed its way into the darkness.

Princess Olivia was so upset. Would she find anything that would help her design a pretty dress? She turned sadly and walked back towards the palace.

All of the animals followed her. What could they find that would help her? Then the clever bumblebee had an idea. She flew high into the sky and disappeared.

Princess Olivia heard a buzzing noise and dried her tears. She looked across the garden, and then jumped up and clapped her hands in delight. 'Mrs Bumblebee! You have got it exactly right!'

The animals all cheered as they
realised what Mrs Bumblebee's plan was.
Of course! The peacock was the most
beautiful thing in the garden.

Its colours would make the most gorgeous dress in the whole land!